A Pride of Is]

C. C. MacApp

Alpha Editions

This edition published in 2024

ISBN 9789362092113

Design and Setting By

Alpha Editions
www.alphaedis.com

Email - info@alphaedis.com

As per information held with us this book is in Public Domain.
This book is a reproduction of an important historical work.
Alpha Editions uses the best technology to reproduce historical work
in the same manner it was first published to preserve its original nature.
Any marks or number seen are left intentionally to preserve.

A Pride of Islands

Alyarsmit clung to the top of a tall swaying hair and squinted toward the ponderous caterpillar-shaped beast way off in the very far distance.

"It's coming this way, all right," he called down to Brusmit, who was leaning against the base of the hair. "It's moved half a length since we first saw it."

"Do you think it sees us yet?" Bru asked uneasily. From up here, six man-lengths above the skin, he looked even shorter and pudgier than he was.

Alyar grinned down at him, then looked toward the front of their own beast. "I think so," he said. "Our eyestalks are up and signaling. The pincers aren't active, though. It must be a friend-beast."

"I don't see how they can recognize each other this far apart," said Bru doubtfully. "We'd better go tell Paboss."

"He sees it." Alyar looked aft to where the leader of the smit clan perched on another hair, a good shout from Alyar's.

"You'd better come down," said Bru. "He clobbered Jorsmit for being in sight, the last time we met another beast."

"He doesn't care when we're this far away." Nevertheless, Alyar climbed down; it wasn't all comfort at the top of a hair, especially when the beast felt you and twitched. "Let's go back there. He might know who it is."

He started through the thick growth of shorter hair, and Bru followed. They moved carefully, listening; it would be nip-and-tuck if only the two of them encountered a fley. They heard a few, detoured around them, eventually reached Paboss's outpost.

The leader was down from the hair, sitting with his back against it, munching dried meat. Three spearmen with him jumped up when they heard Alyar and Bru coming, then, recognizing them, relaxed.

Pabosssmit grunted and gestured toward the joint of meat beside him. "Help yourself." He eyed Alyar keenly. "That you on the hair up forward?"

"Yes, boss. But I made sure I came down in time."

"Don't go showing yourself again before we make contact."

"I won't. Could you tell who it was?"

"Looked like the jaksin beast."

"Oh. We don't fight them, do we?" Alyar was a little disappointed; he'd never been in a fight.

Paboss grinned. "No, but we don't trade with them, either. Pabossjaksin doesn't like me."

Alyar remembered something he'd heard. "Was that where you stole Maboss?"

The grizzled leader filled his thick chest and chuckled. "That's right. Stole her right out from under his nose!" He extended his arms, showing some scars. "Here's where he got me, before I knocked him out. Here's where Ma bit me."

"She *bit* you?"

"Sure. Any girl worth stealing'll put up a fight. I had to haul her along, kicking and screaming, and fight off half the jaksin clan at the same time. It was some party."

Alyar sighed, thinking what it must be like to go raiding. "I'm old enough to have a woman of my own," he mused.

Immediately, Paboss glowered. "Don't you go getting any ideas, hear? I don't want an open war with the jaksins. We've got enough trouble already, with the grans and the kendies." He put a hand tentatively on his club. "You hear?"

"Yes, boss," said Alyar hastily.

During the rest of the day the two beasts halved the distance between them. Near evening, Alyar led Bru, protesting, up to the smit beast's head and down over the edge where they could see forward and remain hidden in the short hair. It was dangerous; the beast might mistake them for fleys and reach up with a pincer-tentacle, which could move fast, considering the size.

When the slow hunching gait stopped and the beast settled down for the night, they went back to the thickly furred spot where the clan lived. Two of the moons were up, and with the excitement of being near another clan, nobody wanted to sleep yet.

Alyar left Bru with an audience of young people who hadn't seen the other beast yet, and went looking for the older men. They were in a clearing, rehashing stories about other clans, especially about the jaksins, which was an old one with a fine repertoire of legends. Maboss had naturally brought the stories with her.

Just now, Paboss was retelling a fascinating, if ridiculous one, about how people had originally come from another world on a beast that could fly.

Alyar sat and listened for a while, then, when the icy evening rain broke up the session, went to his sleeping place in a patch of protecting curly hair. After the first sleep, when it was midnight and dry again, he sneaked to where Bru slept, hissed at him, and drew him away. "Are you game for a little trip?"

"Where? You mean up front again?"

"No. Over to the jaksin beast. Just for fun."

Bru was horrified. "At night? We'd freeze! Anyway, you heard Paboss!"

"We can find something to put on over our own clothes, and wrap our feet in leather. All Paboss said was I mustn't try to steal a girl. Nobody'll miss us for one day, and the beasts will be together by tomorrow noon. We could bring back some kind of souvenirs."

"You must be crazy! What if the jaksins caught us?"

"They'd only haze us a little, if we hadn't done anything. Think of it—besides Paboss and Maboss, only seven smits have ever been to another beast!"

Bundled in extra garments, they sneaked to the curve of the beast's side. Bru acted as if he were going to his own funeral. When they got down to where the hair grew out horizontally, they moved out beyond the short stuff and dropped from one coarse emergent to another; then, finally, to the ground. Apparently no one had heard them. They ran toward the front of the beast, staying as close to the furry belly as possible, for warmth and concealment.

The jaksin beast was due north, half-hidden by the horizon and hard to make out against the background of the tremendous Forest where it had been feeding. Beyond the trees and a little to the right was a volcano, exhaling fiery clouds but not muttering audibly at the moment. East of them was a river; to the west, on the far side of the beasts, another Forest. It was not surprising that the two beasts had met, since they were on a narrow strip of hardened lava between river and Forest.

They traveled in long jumps, gradually closing the distance to the jaksin beast. Near it, they saw that it was awake, with all four front eyestalks and one pair of pincers extended toward them.

They halted out of reach.

"Do you think he'll know we're not jaksins?" Bru whispered.

"I don't think they care *who* lives on them, just so we keep the fleys down. Let him get a good look at us and he'll see we're people."

He was right, but by the time the huge appendages began to retract, the cold was getting through the clothing. They hurried for the shelter of the hair. Warm again, they chewed some of the meat they'd brought along and considered what to do next.

"We'd better go along the ground to the rear," Alyar said. "The men will be mostly near the front, on guard. Back there, there'll only be women and children."

"But we'll be a long way from home. What if the beasts don't come together?"

"Oh, they usually stop and talk, or whatever they do, for three or four days. We'll have a chance to sneak back."

"Why don't we just cut off some hairs right here for souvenirs and go home?"

"Don't you even want to spy on the clan?"

Bru sighed unhappily. "You're not actually going to try to steal a girl, are you?"

"Well—no. But it would be fun, wouldn't it?" His imagination began to percolate. "We're not far from the Warm Ground. That's what the first smit did. He stole a girl and couldn't get home with her, so they lived for a whole season on the Warm Ground until they found a young beast and started their own clan."

"If you've got any crazy ideas like that, you can count me out. People who get lost from their beasts get caught by Demons, or outlaws, or eaten by terrible animals. Next you'll be talking about going to Iron Mountain and fighting the Iron Fley!"

"Huh. The explorers who came back with all those stories probably exaggerated to make themselves look braver. Anyway, all I'm asking you to do is climb on the back end of this beast and spy on the jaksins."

It took the rest of the night to reach the blunt rear end, which had only one pair of eyestalks and one of pincers. They went through the process of letting the beast see them again, so it wouldn't think they were fleys when they began to climb, then picked a low rigid hair to start on.

It was a good four man-lengths up, too much of a jump even in this light gravity for Bru, who missed and floated back to the ground, contorting, while Alyar tried to control his laughter. He uncoiled a rope. "You need a good lively girl to work some of that fat off you," he chuckled as he hauled Bru up.

Panting, Bru pulled himself onto the hair. "You'll get me killed before I ever have a chance to get married. Do you think they heard us?"

"No. We haven't heard *them* yet, and they're bound to be jabbering like women always are." He coiled the rope and they began to climb.

When they were halfway up, there were squeaks and rumbles below them. They stopped, holding their breaths, while the tentacle curled toward a spot only thirty or forty man-lengths away and the great claw began digging at the fur. Evidently something itched there; and in a few moments, they did hear the screech of a hurt fley. They resumed climbing.

When the skin was level enough to walk on, they began hearing voices—the giggling of girls and the drier chatter of older women, but no men's voices. They crept forward, parted the hair very carefully, and peered out.

They must have found the quarters of a very important family, for the clearing was freshly cut and expensive woven rugs covered the skin. The walls were evenly trimmed, with several hung paintings. Sleeping places had been cut into one side and lined with soft leather from the underparts of fleys.

Alyar had only a glance for all this luxury, though, for within two man-lengths of him sat a pair of eminently stealable girls. Temptation battered at him. One, evidently the older sister, was well muscled and lithe, but plump enough to have curves everywhere. The other was beautiful too, but more slender. They had the black hair and tawny smooth skin of the jaksins. Each wore a short lounging skirt of dainty leather which left few secrets.

Prudence, overwhelmed, hardly put up a fight.

Alyar maneuvered Bru carefully back until he could whisper. He ignored the desperate protests. "Shut up. All you have to do is stay here and wait for me, and when you hear a commotion, screech like a fley. You can do that much, can't you?"

Bru, groaning, finally nodded.

A length from the clearing, Alyar chose a young hair-shoot and put the point of his spear in the tender spot at its base. He jabbed with all his weight, then dove for the clearing. The beast's involuntary twitch came as he broke into the open.

The women were scrambling to their feet, with cries of "Beastquake!" and right on schedule Bru cut loose with a fine series of fley screeches. In the confusion nobody noticed that Alyar was a stranger until he scooped up the two girls, one under each arm, and jumped for the fur.

It was hard going, with both of them grabbing at hairs to hold them back, scratching him, and in general being uncooperative. He was panting when he reached Bru.

"Here!" he gasped, considerately tossing him the slender one who'd be easier to carry. "This one's yours."

The plump one knew by now what was happening. Slyly, she went limp until Alyar relaxed; then she twisted suddenly and got her teeth at his left shoulder. He yelled as she took out a respectable divot of flesh, and spun her around so she couldn't reach him again.

There was much screaming behind them, but no pursuit yet. Alyar urged Bru to the base of the nearest eyestalk. "Start climbing!"

"But we'll be trapped up there!"

"No, we won't. Go on!"

They were ten man-lengths up before a few old men and a crowd of women and children appeared at the base of the stalk. Seeing Alyar's spear-hand free part of the time, none acted anxious to follow them.

Now they were high enough to be hurt in a fall, and the girls had prudently stopped struggling. Alyar's twisted her head and glared at him. "My father will feed you to the fleys!"

Alyar grinned. "He'll have to catch us first. What's your name?"

"Go to hell."

He let go of the scale he was clinging to with his right hand, and pinched her in a vulnerable spot. She shrieked.

"If I have to keep pinching you," he said, "we'll probably fall. You'd better tell me your name."

She hesitated, then said icily, "Janeejaksin."

"Hm. You seem to be rich girls. You wouldn't be the Paboss's daughters, would you?"

Janee wouldn't answer, but the other girl did, rather cordially. "Yes, and my name's Marisujaksin. Are you going to steal us and make smits of us?"

"They'll never get off this eyestalk," Janee said scornfully.

Alyar motioned Bru higher. The figures around the base grew tiny and the stalk tapered to only half the girth of a man. It swayed a little, and they moved around to what would be the upper side if it bent.

Shouts could be heard now from farther forward; undoubtedly the fighters would arrive soon. Bru looked nervously in that direction. "What are we going to do—bargain with them?"

"No. Listen carefully. You know about people riding a pincer. We're going to get one up here, and when it's close enough, jump onto it and ride it to the ground." Alyar grinned at the protests, put his spear-point between two scales, and jabbed.

In a minute the eyestalk began to bend ponderously downward. Far below they could see the pincer-tentacle starting up to meet it.

"Be lively, now!" Alyar warned.

It took a while for the pincer to arrive. They jumped from two man-lengths, landed on the slanting horny surface, and slid. Alyar, hanging onto

Janee with one arm, managed to get the other around a small prong. He threw a glance toward Bru and saw that he'd made out all right too. They waited.

Even though the irritation had stopped, the beast was going through with the scratching after hauling all that weight to such a height. The tip of the pincer sawed deliberately at the place Alyar had jabbed, and then they started down.

The movement was faster than it looked from a distance; still, it was a long way to the ground. Partway down, the beast saw them and the claw halted. They crouched while the stalk bent to bring the immense eye directly over them, but evidently the creature was only wondering what they were up to now, for after a while the tentacle started down again.

Three man-lengths from the ground they jumped, landed, and bounded away out of reach.

Men, shouting, were clinging to long hairs, but nobody was climbing the eyestalk. Perhaps no one wanted to imitate the novel descent. Closer shouts indicated a group coming down through the fur.

"What now?" Bru asked.

It was a reasonable question. Even if they dared go home, they'd have to parallel the whole length of this beast and could hardly avoid interception. Alyar and Bru had discarded their extra clothing, while the girls were almost bare, so warmth would be an absolute necessity when night came.

Alyar looked northward toward the volcano. The Warm Ground was supposed to surround it for some distance; maybe they could reach that before night. There wasn't much time to ponder. Men were already dropping to the ground. He picked up Janee and ran for the nearest cover, which was the Forest. "Come on, we can't stay here!"

Bru didn't have to carry Marisu—she was evidently coming along regardless, even though she wailed a little—so he was able to keep up. "We're not going into the Forest, are we?" he panted.

"Just into the edge to get out of sight. Then we'll decide."

They were still a medium shout ahead when they came to the first colossal uprights; trunks so thick it would take a man many breaths to run around one; towering so high one tended to forget there were any tops. In between were smaller plants, some with flowers, that formed a thicket as dense as fur.

Alyar paused, thinking of the stories he'd heard about the Forest. But there was no doubt about how real the danger was behind them, so he held his spear at the ready and plunged into the growth.

Janee opened her mouth to scream, and he hastily muffled it with his hand. "Do you want to attract every Demon in the Forest?"

Her eyes widened and she quit struggling.

He listened to the shouts from outside, then pointed north. "That way."

Bru gaped. "But that's away from home!"

"We can't go home yet. Anyway, the jaksins'll expect us to. They're moving south already. Hear them?"

Inside the Forest, in the deep shade, there was less vegetation so that they were able to move easily. Whenever Janee looked ready to scream, Alyar pretended to see or hear something, and by the time she was wise to that, they were out of earshot.

Their luck didn't last long, though. They heard a sound, whirled, and saw a small being on a branch, watching them with malevolent yellow eyes.

The girls whimpered, and Bru moaned, "A Demon!"

It had taken a strange shape, with four limbs and one other appendage that looked like a tentacle. It was covered with short black fur, very thick and fine. Just now it had a set of claws for clinging to the tree.

Before they could run, it opened its mouth and uttered a curse, which sounded like "Meow!"

"Let's get out of here!" Bru whispered.

Alyar knew better. "There's no use running; we're already cursed. The only thing is to try to appease it."

"Maybe we could give it the girls?"

Alyar wavered. He'd become quite attached to Janee, though he was a little tired of being bitten and scratched, and he *had* gone to a lot of trouble to get her. "Let's try meat first," he decided.

He got a small piece out of his pouch and extended it on the end of his spear. Heart pounding, he moved closer. The Demon tensed as if to jump at them, then seemed to change its mind. It wrinkled its nose (which Alyar hoped was a sign of favor) and finally stretched out its head and took the meat. It chewed daintily and swallowed.

Alyar let out his breath. Nothing was guaranteed, of course, but possibly....

The Demon said, "Meow," in a different tone.

Carefully, they edged toward the open. After a few steps Bru began to run. Immediately, there was a loud "MEOW!" and he stopped.

In a moment the Demon came into sight, walking on the ground. Alyar noticed that it had ungrown the claws. As he looked (no doubt reading his thought) it grew them again, stretched out its two front limbs, lengthened its body, and yawned.

They started on, but weren't able to make much time until they found that the Demon wanted to be carried.

At the edge of the Forest, it was disappointing to see how little distance they had covered. The nearest end of the jaksin beast, hunching slowly away now toward the smit beast, was still within three shouts. However, no jaksins were in sight.

Again, Alyar hesitated; troubles seemed to be piling up. Still, he didn't see any choice. "We'll have to go to the Warm Ground," he said.

The girls sobbed a little, and he frowned at them. "*Now* what's wrong?"

"There are terrible outlaws there, and Demons, and—and things."

His patience ran out. "To hell with them! We already have one Demon; do you think it's going to share us with everything on the planet? Come on!"

Janee didn't insist on being carried now; evidently she felt compromised enough to come along. They hurried, stopping only once to finish up their food. They were thirsty, but Hot Water was supposed to come up out of the Warm Ground, and anyway they could wait for the evening rains.

It was dusk, and already beginning to drizzle, when they noticed that the ground under their feet was warm.

This was mostly hardened lava, sloping upward toward the volcano, but with small streams and patches of vegetation.

Before they found a good place to stop for the night, Bru pointed ahead. "Look! That glow!"

They went forward cautiously until they could see what must be a Fire, with people sitting around it. Fascinated, Alyar went closer. Suddenly he heard the girls scream, and simultaneously two pairs of rough hands seized him from behind. He wrenched desperately, throwing himself and the two husky men around, but not getting free. More came shouting, to help pin him down and tie him with ropes. It sounded as if Bru and the girls were being similarly treated.

A man who acted like the leader came running from the Fire. "What have we got here? Scouts?" He began directing squads of spearmen as if he expected an attack. "Two women with them? Funny. All right, you—who're you spying for?"

"What are you talking about?" Alyar demanded, as indignantly as his position allowed. "We're from the smit clan and we're—trying to get home," he finished lamely.

"Clan? From a beast? What are you doing up here, then?"

"We came to keep warm."

"Keep warm? Why didn't you build a Fire?"

"I—we don't believe in Fires."

Laughter arose. "Let him up," the leader said. "He must be telling the truth. Only a fley-eater would be so ignorant."

They took off some of the ropes. Alyar rubbed at various bruises and abrasions, wondering whether he and Bru would be killed or made slaves. The outlaws would surely keep the girls. He wondered whether the Demon were going to give up its property so easily.

As if in answer to the thought, it came strolling into the light, and the leader made a sign nervously. "Damn! A black cat! Is it yours?"

"A black what? It captured us in the Forest."

"It ... captured you? In the Forest? Then it's a real Demon!"

"Of course! How can you be so ignorant?"

"And you're still alive?"

"It hasn't hurt us yet, but it won't let us get away and it makes us carry it. I think we're uncursed right now. I'm not sure; I sort of lost track."

The man gulped and faced the Demon. "Please forgive us, Demon. We didn't know these people were yours."

The Demon looked at him scornfully and uttered a curse. People moved away, except one young spearman who stood his ground. "It—it sounds just like a cat," he quavered.

The leader knocked him spinning with the sweep of a forearm. "Of course it sounds like a cat! How do you think it would sound when it's in cat form? Do you expect it to speak ingils to us?" He beckoned to several women.

"Bring food for the Demon, and offerings of iron and jewels!" He glanced at the four captives, and added, as an afterthought, "Better feed its slaves, too."

Cooked meat was easy to chew, but it tasted odd, and the fruit was completely baffling. Still, they were filling.

The outlaw leader eyed the Demon, which had pre-empted Janee's ample lap. "Where is it taking you?"

Alyar didn't want to admit how little he knew of the nature of things, so he said the most awesome thing he could think of. "To Iron Mountain."

There were gasps. "Oh, what unfortunate people you are!" the leader said. Then, eagerly, "When will you go?"

Alyar thought he'd better press his luck. "It wants us to start right away. It only pretends to be asleep like that, to see if we're obedient. Er—I seem to have gotten turned around. Which way is Iron Mountain from here?"

The man pointed with alacrity. "That way! A third of the distance around the volcano. Here, we'll help you get loaded up."

The girls were festooned with necklaces and pendants of rare stones, while Bru and Alyar toted the food and the oddments of iron. The outlaws had hastily gathered a fabulous treasure of the metal—whole spearheads, and even a knife, of it!

Alyar waved and smiled at the outlaws just before they were out of sight, then turned north.

"We'll go upcountry," he said. "They won't look for us there. I'm not sure they won't follow; they probably don't know what this Demon will do any more than we do." He saw some huge rocks not far away, with bushes growing on top. "Let's climb up there."

When they were halfway to the rocks, incredible good fortune struck. The Demon with one hurried "Meow!" scrambled away from Janee and ran back toward the outlaw camp.

"Come on!" Alyar exclaimed. "Maybe we can get out of its circle of influence!"

They climbed the rocks and found they could see the Fire. Presently they knew the Demon had arrived there, for the distant figures scattered. Moments later, faint laments drifted to them.

They spent the rest of the night awake and watchful. "The outlaws will surely be after us now," Bru said, "to get back all this treasure."

"Marisu and I want to be near our clan," said Janee. "Even if—" she blushed—"you make smits out of us, the two beasts would meet once in a while and we could visit."

Alyar looked eastward, where numerous glows marked other outlaw camps. The volcano was a barrier to the north. The outlaws would bar the way to the south, expecting them to head home to the beasts. The only direction left was west, and he found that it pleased him.

"I guess we'll just have to visit Iron Mountain," he said. "Then we'll be such heroes that Pabosses smit and jaksin will have to forgive us."

The girls looked at him with awe while Bru moaned.

When the sun came up they could see the northern end of the Forest, south of which the jaksin beast had been feeding. Past it, surprisingly visible from this altitude, were the two beasts, head-to-head with eyestalks touching.

The Forest ran up close to the steep side of the volcano, leaving only a narrow pass. Beyond that was the river which, turning south, passed the two beasts. Farther up the river, according to legend, was Iron Mountain.

They stayed long enough to see what kind of animals prowled the country and to lay out a course, then climbed down and got started. They walked all day with only a few halts and some minor adventures with strange animals, then found another high place to spend the night. In the darkness they spotted a single Fire west of them. The next morning they detoured around that spot, and entered the narrow pass. Before noon they stood looking down at the river.

The canyon was deeper and wider than Alyar could have imagined, and there was more water at the bottom. The country ahead, though, was so rough that it seemed the easiest way was to climb down and go along the river. It took them half the afternoon to get down.

Not very long after that, Alyar put out his hand. "Wait! I hear voices!"

They were men's voices and seemed to be coming downstream.

He pushed the other three to a hiding place behind some rocks and bushes. When the owners of the voices came into sight around a turn, he gasped. They weren't walking, but riding on the water itself, in something like a big dish.

"Magicians!" Bru whispered.

Two of the men (there were seven) were stroking the water with some kind of wands, flattened at the ends. They acted as if they were fleeing from something, talking in low voices and staring back upstream. Just before they came opposite, it caught up with them.

The first thing Alyar heard was a loud voice, distorted and with an odd accent. He had trouble making out the repeated words. "Halt or I'll shoot. Advance and be recognized. Halt or I'll shoot. Advance—"

The thing came into sight—flying! He gripped Bru's shoulder. "The Iron Fley!"

It was made of the kind of iron that didn't rust, and had only eight legs, not ten. All of them were folded to its sides except one with a larger, oblong foot; that one was extended toward the fugitives.

When they saw it, they jumped out of their dish and sank into the water.

"Halt or I'll shoot," said the Iron Fley again, then hurled its spell. The dish shattered abruptly into small bits and a hissing cloud burst out of the water.

The terrible creature circled over the floating fragments for a few minutes, then flew off upstream. When it was gone the seven magicians appeared, climbing out of the river on the far side.

"Damn it!" said one. "A good boot lost, and not a bit of iron. I *told* you we ought to wait for night!"

"It doesn't make any difference," said another gloomily. "It's always on watch. Nobody's gotten away with any iron for three or four seasons."

"Well," said Alyar, after the magicians had straggled off down the river, "now we've seen it. It certainly put a powerful spell on that floating dish, but it didn't hurt the magicians. Maybe if we're careful it won't bother us."

They followed the twisting canyon and eventually began to hear a roaring noise ahead. It turned out to be the water falling over a cliff, and to go any farther they had to climb out of the canyon again. When they were on top they could see, ahead of them, what was undoubtedly Iron Mountain.

Parts of it were broken or rusted, but most of it was the non-rusting kind. Its shape was a surprise. It didn't look like a mountain, but something made by giants, broken off and stuck into the ground.

It was wonderful to stand here, beholding the mightiest magic in the entire world. Still, Alyar wasn't satisfied. He felt he must go closer, even—possibly—touch it.

"You'd better stay here. Bru, if anything happens to me, take the girls and run. You can get back to the beasts by going down the river."

Bru was dismayed. "Don't go any closer! You saw what happened to the magicians' dish!"

"They were trying to steal iron." He unloaded the metal he was carrying, smiled at them, and went on.

He'd only covered a hundred man-lengths or so when he heard the distorted voice, coming from over his head. He looked up, then stood rooted as the Iron Fley came spiraling down toward him. He tried to think the purest, most serene thoughts he could, though the fervent wish to be somewhere else kept intruding.

The thing paused a few lengths away. "Advance and be recognized," it said.

He took a faltering hop forward. "Halt or I'll shoot," it said, and he stopped.

"Advance."

He did.

"Halt."

He did.

Finally he was very close to it, and he waited for a spell to hit him.

"Name, rank, and serial number," it demanded. Then, as he was silent "Speak or I'll shoot."

"I—I'm Alyarsmit! I don't think I'm rank, and I don't know what a serial number is."

"Friend or foe?"

"F-friend. I haven't stolen anything. Just some girls."

The thing made a buzzing sound. "You speak, and you have the requisite number of limbs, and one head. Are you human?"

"Y-yes, I'm human."

"Name?"

"Alyarsmit."

"Smith? Smith?" It buzzed some more. "There was a Colonel John Smith on the roster. Are you his descendant?"

"Yes," Alyar hazarded.

"Mr. Smith, sir, Robojeep twenty-seven four nine reporting. All other jeeps inactivated, sir. No ship's personnel or other passengers accounted for in the last three hundred and seventy-four planetary cycles. Damage to ship unrepairable without human direction. Sporadic raids by savages, possibly degenerate humans, repelled successfully. Will you assume manual control, sir?"

Alyar stuck with "Yes."

"Very well, sir." The Iron Fley descended and walked toward him on six of its legs, then squatted.

He stared at its back. Actually, it didn't have one; it was hollowed out from the top, and in the hollow were—seats! Four of them!

Unable to mistake the meaning, he climbed in and sat down. Nothing happened for a while. Then the creature began to buzz again. "Have you forgotten the controls, sir? The lever on the left is for elevation; the other one for horizontal motion. Would you prefer vocal control?"

"N-no, this is all right."

"Very good, sir." The buzz stopped.

The levers were just in front of him. Gingerly, he reached out and gave the left-hand one a twitch, then yelled and let go of it as they shot upward. They stopped, and he tried again gently. They rose more smoothly.

He experimented with the other and moved forward, backward, and to the sides. He lowered to a height where he was less frightened. "Er—Fley?"

"You spoke, sir?"

"I can go wherever I want?"

"Except into obvious danger, sir. I'm programmed to avoid that."

Alyar flew toward where he'd left his companions. They lay face down, lamenting, Janee loudest of all. He eyed her posterior, and Bru's, with some misgivings. The Fley's seats were a little skimpy.

He landed beside them, cleared his throat, and waited until they raised dumfounded faces.

"Get in," he said.

Against feeble protests from the others, he maneuvered the creature (which preferred to be called "Jeep") toward Iron Mountain. When they were close

Jeep woke up, buzzed, and hovered while a great doorway slid open. It carried the four, clinging together, into the hollow blackness within.

Then, quite suddenly—even though the door slid shut behind them—it was light as day inside.

What a cave! Cylindrical, all of fifty man-lengths across, it slanted down until it must reach far below ground. Far down there, where Jeep was taking them, were some level platforms.

As soon as they settled on one, a terrible, huge, clanking monster, also of non-rusting iron, flew toward them. They huddled while it spoke. "Mr. Smith, sir, Roborepairunit seventeen reporting. Ship's power and drive in order. Unable to complete hull repairs, or repair other working and scouting units, without cannibalizing part of living quarters. Do I have Mr. Smith's permission to proceed?"

Alyar gulped several times, and got out "Yes."

"Thank you, sir. The job will require arc cutting and welding and other high-temperature processes. Will you be here very long?"

"We hope not."

"Very well, sir. I'll begin as soon as you leave."

They sat for a while, wondering what to do. Finally Alyar said, "Jeep?"

"Sir?"

"Would we be permitted to leave?"

"At once, sir."

More buzzing, and the door opened again.

As they flew away, Jeep said, "Sir, Roborepair wants to know whether to repair ship in its present position or move it elsewhere."

Alyar was beginning to feel more confident. "In its present position, I think. For now."

As they turned south, Janee began to sniffle.

"What now?" he demanded.

"I miss my Demon."

Alyar turned to Bru. "Isn't that just like a woman? She wants a Demon again!"

She raised her head and glared at him. "He was cute and soft, and he cuddled against me and made happy sounds. You tamed the Iron Fley, and if you really loved me, you could surely handle one little fluffy Demon!"

Alyar let Jeep stop and hang there while he tried to cope with the effrontery of it. After all he'd been through, stealing her, to have her suggest that he go into more danger just to satisfy her crazy whim!

His hands reached out for the levers again. Shaking his head dazedly, he started northeast to look for the outlaws.

Some time later, they were headed south again, Janee's Demon asleep in her lap. Jeep was loggy with iron and other treasures extorted from various bands of outlaws. In the two rear seats, Bru and Marisu were holding hands.

He was startled to see two more beasts hunching up from the south, beyond the smits and jaksins. Four of them together at one time!

When they circled down, they found Pabossmit on his hair, scowling southward. He cringed when he saw the Iron Fley, then managed to look both dumfounded and furious when he recognized Alyar and Bru.

"You young hoodlums! I'm glad that thing caught you! Look there—those are the grans and the kendies coming, and Pabossjaksin's so mad he'll join them against us!" His face softened into the start of a grin as he sized up the two girls, but then hardened again. "I hope you're proud of yourselves, getting your whole clan killed or made slaves!"

Alyar started toward a clearing. "Come on down, Paboss. We've got so much magic now, we could laugh at all the clans in the world." And, to Jeep, "Jeep, can we bring Iron Mountain over here and fly it around and show these savages they better behave?"

"A bloodless demonstration? Certainly, sir. I'll go aloft at once and radio."

The four stood in a clearing, with awed smits around them at a respectful distance. Paboss came pushing through the hair, as awed as any, but less scared.

"Tamed the Iron Fley!" He began to guffaw. "Stole Pabossjaksin's own two daughters! Haw, haw! Young man, when I retire...." His eyes covered Janee approvingly, then turned back to Alyar. "You're wounded! What—oh, toothmarks!" He laughed some more. "Didn't I say any girl worth stealing would put up a fight?"

Alyar happened to be looking toward Bru, who had his own knot of admirers. Marisu was standing a little behind him, as a bride should. At Paboss's words, she frowned and her eyes fixed on Bru's smooth shoulder. Her gaze grew more intent. She moved slowly forward, her eyes crossing as they remained on the spot.

Closer....

Closer....

Bru yelled.